LITTLE MIS
and t...

originated by Roger Hargreaves

Written by Alice Downes
Illustrated by JT Morrow

MR. MEN **LITTLE MISS**
by Roger Hargreaves

MR. MEN™ LITTLE MISS™
Copyright © 2014 THOIP (a Sanrio® company).
All rights reserved.
Used Under License.
www.mrmenlittlemiss.net

SIL-5018

PSS!
PRICE STERN SLOAN

An Imprint of Penguin Group (USA) LLC
Text and illustrations copyright © 2014 by THOIP (a Sanrio® company).
Little Miss Splendid is a trademark of THOIP (a Sanrio® company). All rights reserved.
Published by Price Stern Sloan, a division of Penguin Young Readers Group,
345 Hudson Street, New York, New York 10014.
PSS! is a registered trademark of Penguin Group (USA) LLC. Manufactured in China.
The publisher does not have any control over and does not assume any
responsibility for author or third-party websites or their content.

ISBN 978-0-8431-8242-2   10 9 8 7 6 5 4 3 2

Have you heard the fairy tale about the Beauty and the Beast? Well, it turns out something similar happened in Happyland!

Once upon a time, in a land far away—well, in Happyland, that is—there lived a smug little beauty called . . . Little Miss Splendid.

She was perfectly splendid—or at least she thought she was.

One day, Little Miss Splendid went for a walk in the dark, quiet woods.

She was thinking about how magnificently splendid she was, and before she knew it, she was lost! Suddenly it started to rain and thunder.

"Oh dear!" she said. "My shoes! My splendid hat!"

Just then, she saw a castle in the distance.

Little Miss Splendid let herself in. All the rooms were beautiful, but there was no one there.

She saw a bright light beneath a closed door, so she pushed open the door, and do you know what she did?

She SCREAMED!

Standing there, minding his own business in his castle, was a huge, hairy beast.

"Are you okay?" he asked Little Miss Splendid.

Little Miss Splendid screamed again.

"There's no need to scream," said the Beast kindly. "I just want to make sure you're all right."

Little Miss Splendid screamed again.

"Why don't you come close to the fire and warm up?" suggested the Beast very, very gently.

And with that, Little Miss Splendid screamed once more and ran from the room.

First, Little Miss Splendid tried to hide in the castle's kitchen, but the Beast found her.

Then, Little Miss Splendid tried to hide in one of the bedrooms, but the Beast found her.

Finally, Little Miss Splendid hid behind a sofa in the library.

"Please stop running and screaming," begged the Beast.

She screamed again.

"I won't hurt you," said the Beast. "I've been so lonely, and I'm delighted you came by. I'd like to be friends." The Beast became smitten with Little Miss Splendid, despite her being so difficult.

She finally calmed down a bit.

"I don't have any beastly friends," she answered, though her voice did soften.

The Beast took her softened tone as an opportunity to tell her about himself.

I bet you're wondering how the Beast became the Beast, too!

"I haven't always been this way," he said. "Years ago, I was put under a spell by a witch who turned me into a beast. Ever since then, I've been ashamed to leave my castle."

Do you think Little Miss Splendid felt sorry for him?

Not at all!

"That's indeed a sad story," she said, turning her nose up, "but I really must go."

"Please stay," the Beast begged. "Your timing is as splendid as your sparkling red shoes. Tomorrow, this nasty spell wears off, and we are throwing a banquet to celebrate. Will you come as my special guest?"

Little Miss Splendid thought it over. One of the things she loved most in the world was being the guest of honor at parties and important events.

"Okay, you Beast," answered Little Miss Splendid, looking away. "I will come to your party. But I have high expectations!"

When Little Miss Splendid arrived at the party the next day, she thought she looked more splendid than anyone else there.

She also thought the party was just so-so. The food was average. The setting was kind of okay. The Beast was still a beast.

When the Beast saw Little Miss Splendid, he ran toward her.

"I'm so happy you're here! You look absolutely splendid," he said.

Little Miss Splendid ignored the Beast. She looked around to see if there was anyone she knew at the party.

Little Miss Chatterbox was keeping Little Miss Shy company.

Mr. Strong was carrying a giant cake into the dining room. Mr. Fussy was sweeping up the crumbs he left.

Little Miss Splendid thought everyone helping one another out was perfectly dull.

"I'm leaving, Beast," she said.

And with that, she spun on her red heels and walked out.

"Please, don't leave," the heartbroken Beast called from the castle window.

Little Miss Splendid ignored him.

Then Little Miss Splendid heard a loud BANG! She turned and looked through the open window into the ballroom.

The banquet guests cheered, and there were balloons everywhere.

And do you know what she saw?

In the center of the ballroom, she saw the Beast suddenly transformed into . . .

Mr. Perfect!

Little Miss Splendid quickly realized her mistake, so she ran back inside. How could she have passed on Mr. Perfect?

Being the perfect person that he was, the Beast-turned-Mr. Perfect gave Little Miss Splendid a hug.

And they lived happily ever after.

Or did they?